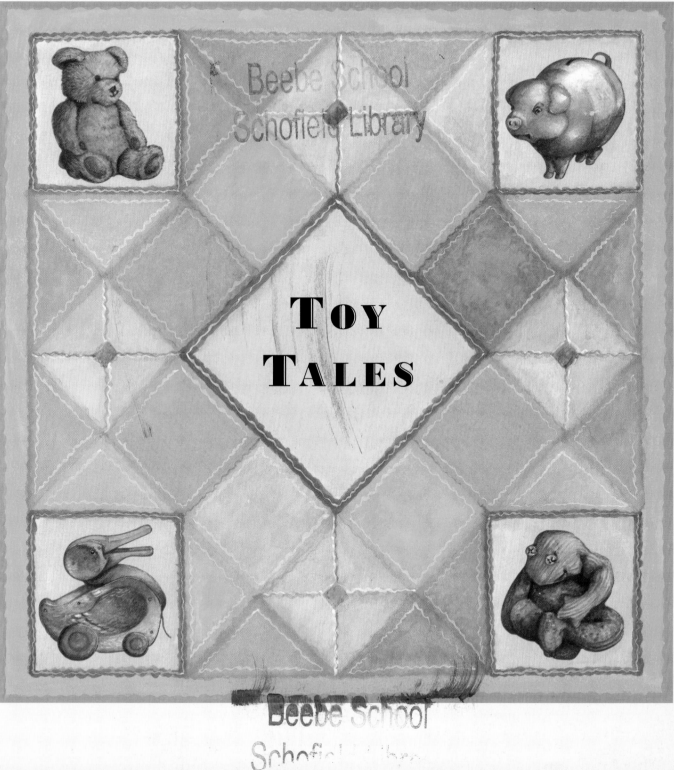

# TOY
# TALES

The stories in this book were first published separately in Great Britain as
*The Tale of Bear, The Tale of Frog, The Tale of Duck,* and *The Tale of Pig* by
Doubleday, a division of Transworld Publishers, in 1994.
The collection *Toy Tales* was first published in Great Britain by Picture Corgi.
Corgi Books are published by Transworld Publishers,
a division of the Random House Group Ltd.
Printed in Singapore
First American edition, 2000
1 3 5 7 9 10 8 6 4 2

Library of Congress Cataloging-in-Publication Data

Cooper, Helen (Helen F.)
   Toy tales / Helen Cooper.— 1st American ed.
      p.   cm.
   "A Sunburst book."
   "The stories in this book were first published separately in Great
Britain as The tale of Bear, The tale of Frog, The tale of Duck, and
The tale of Pig . . ."
   Summary: Even after they each have a mishap, a young boy still
loves his special teddy bear, stuffed frog, wooden duck, and piggy bank.
   ISBN 0-374-47944-5
   [1. Toys—Fiction.   2. Animals—Fiction.   3. Stories in rhyme.]
I. Title.
PZ8.3.C785 Tt 2000
[E]—dc21                                                    99-56713

# Helen Cooper

# Toy Tales

A Sunburst Book

Farrar, Straus and Giroux

This
book belongs to

. . . . . . . . . . . . . . . . . . . . . . . . . . . . .

. . . . . . . . . . . . . . . . . . . . . . . . . . . . . . .

# CONTENTS

*For*
Heather, Hugo, Anik and Sharon

# Bear's Tale

Whatever Timothy had to do,
Bear came, too.
So wherever Bear was, there was Tim
next to him.

But Bear was feeling very scruffy,
fur and feet were getting mucky.
Bear was worried – would Tim care?
Would Tim want a dirty old Bear?

Bear was snuggled up asleep
when naughty Cat came in to play.
She left him tangled in the sheets,
she hid him there . . . on washing day!

Poor Bear, trapped in the washing machine,
sploshing around in the soap and steam.
"Won't someone help me?" shouted Bear.
But Mom didn't hear him. Didn't she care?

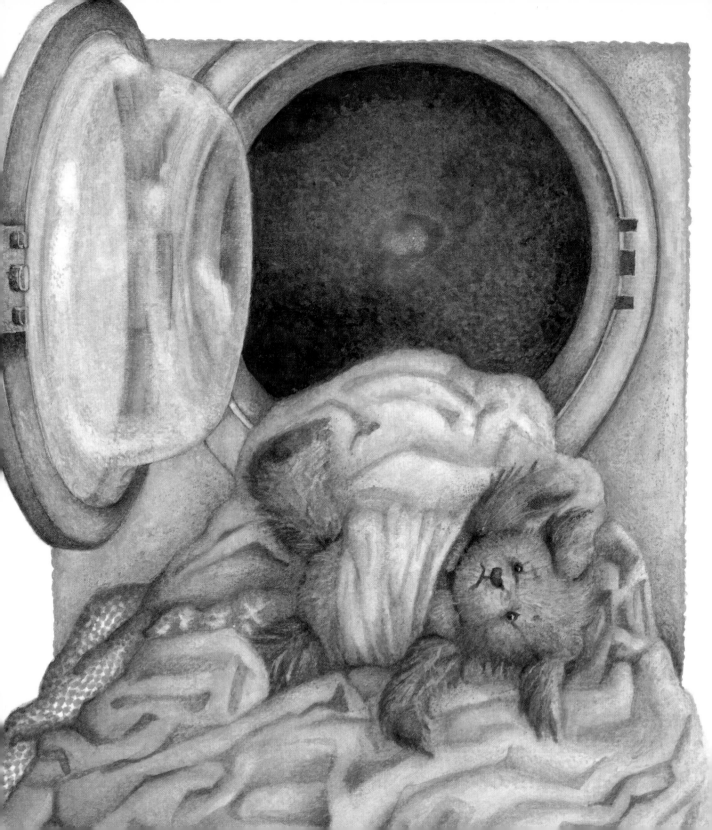

"Oh no!" said Mom when she opened the door
and Bear fell out on the kitchen floor.
He was soaked to his stuffing, and very scared
that Tim wouldn't want a soggy old Bear.

His fur was bedraggled, all matted and wet.
Pinned by his ears, he tried not to stretch.
But he couldn't *help* stretching – would Tim care?
Would Tim mind a saggy old Bear?

But when he was combed and his seams
were stitched,
he looked pretty good, he had to admit.
Then he thought again and worried some more . . .
What if Tim liked him better as he was before?

Tim was most surprised to find
a clean Bear, but he didn't mind.
Dirty old paws or fluffy gold hair,
he loved his squashy old, saggy old Bear.

# Frog's Tale

Timothy's frog, all stuffed with rice,
small and floppy but very nice,
sat at the end of the bed one night,
heard a squeak and got a fright.

Into the room came a family of mice.
They nibbled the toy who was stuffed with rice.
Rice leaked out all over the bed.
"Won't someone mend me?" poor Frog said.

Then Cat crept in and she sniffed about.
Frog smelled of mouse, so she carried him out.
Cat was racing. Frog was shaking
and bouncing and bumping . . .
. . . and rice kept escaping!

Frog was soon so empty that
the game was over now for Cat.
She let him drop and went outside.
"Won't someone help me?" poor Frog cried.

But Tim found rice near the bedroom chair.
He followed the trail right down the stairs.
And there was Frog, completely flat,
sprawling across the dusty mat.

"We can't put rice back in," said Tim.
"The mice will come and nibble him."
So they stuffed him full with snippets of rag.
They filled every space, so he didn't sag.

They mended the hole that was nibbled by mice.
They sewed him strong and tied him tight.
Frog isn't floppy and scared anymore.
He's bigger and braver than he was before.

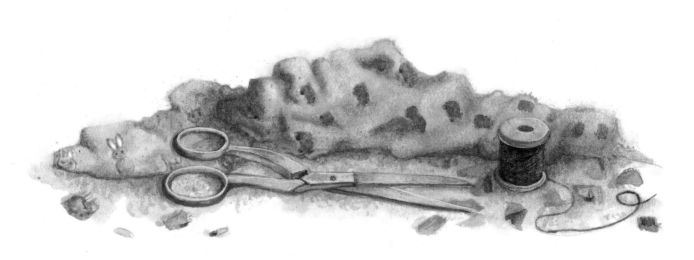

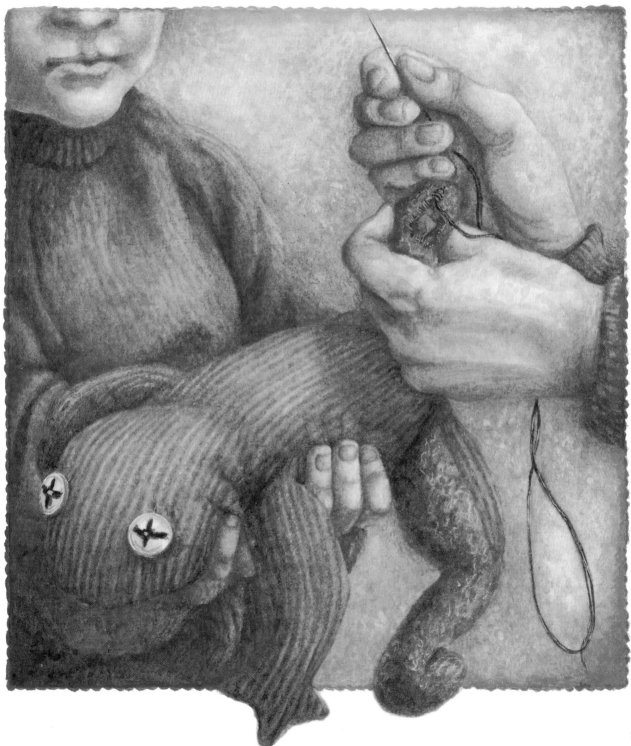

And if those mice come back one night,
Frog will give them quite a fright.
They'll soon discover their mistake
and see what a difference a stuffing can make.

# Duck's Tale

Duck was speedy, Duck was quick.
He crossed the carpet lickety-split;
he won every race, knew every trick,
for Duck was the fastest toy.

45

Engine, tractor, blue dump truck,
none of the others could quite keep up.
No one could race as fast as Duck,
for Duck was the fastest toy.

Always the leader, never the last –
"Stop!" cried Tim. "You're going too fast!"
Duck didn't hear, he whizzed straight past –
Whoooossh! went the fastest toy.

On and on, toward the stairs.
Would he dare to race down there?
Of course he would – he wasn't scared . . .
Be careful, fastest toy!

But Duck found out that stairs are steep,
not meant for wheels, but made for feet.
Clickety, clackety, rattle bang thump.
Daredevil Duck fell . . . with a

B U M P!

Duck was broken, Duck had crashed,
his wheels could not be mended.
His head was chipped, his beak was bashed,
his racing days had ended.

Duck missed the fun, after his fall.
He couldn't race, he could only crawl,
and he missed his old friends most of all,
now he wasn't the fastest toy.

But look! His racing days are back.
He's waving a flag at the end of the track.
When the winner comes by, it's

"QUACK QUACK QUACK!

Three cheers for the fastest toy!"

# Pig's Tale

The Pig on the shelf,
sits all by himself,
guarding Tim's money
in his big fat tummy.

63

Chubby old Pig
is smug with pride
when he feels Tim's money
slipping inside.

Pig looks down on the other toys.
*He's* too important to play with small boys.
He sits alone and thinks of the money
that rattles around in his big fat tummy.

But here comes Cat.
She gives Pig a tap.
He wibbles,
    and wobbles
        and falls . . . and is . . .

# SMASHED!

His treasure is rolling all over the floor.
Tim picks it up and runs to the door.
Is he going to spend the money
while Pig lies there with a broken tummy?

Poor old Pig! He's worried that they
will pick up the pieces and throw them away.
He doesn't know Tim has spent the money
on special glue to mend his tummy!

Tim and his mother collect all the bits,
glue them together and make sure they fit.
Pig feels better, but something's not right . . .
the money won't go in – the slot is too tight!

But look! Pig smiles, and he didn't before.
Perhaps it's because Tim plays with him
more.
Pig doesn't mind his empty tummy –
games are much more fun than money.